I0557109

ASYMMETRICAL SPIRITUAL WARFARE

Battlefield Manual for Soldiers of Light

SAM HAGER

Unless otherwise indicated, all Scripture quotations are from
The ESV® Bible (The Holy Bible, English Standard Version®), ©
2001 by Crossway, a publishing ministry of Good News
Publishers. Used by permission.
All rights reserved.

Scripture taken from the New King James Version®.
Copyright © 1982 by Thomas Nelson. Used by permission.
All rights reserved.

Scripture quotations marked (NLT) are taken from the Holy
Bible, New Living Translation, copyright © 1996, 2004, 2007 by
Tyndale House Foundation. Used by permission of Tyndale
House Publishers, Inc.,
Carol Stream, Illinois 60188.
All rights reserved.

Copyright © 2024 Treign Publishing
All rights reserved.

ISBN: 978-1-7378124-3-2

CONTENTS

Foreword

It is with great joy that I am able to write the foreword to the book that you now hold. Spiritual Warfare has continued to be an intriguing topic over the last few years. I believe it is because of the times and seasons we are now living in awaiting the arrival of our Lord Jesus Christ!

The following pages are written as a primer for the Body of Christ as they exercise their spiritual authority in Christ to assuage the onslaught of the enemy on behalf of the lost. Understanding our authority in Christ is vital to any believer if they are going to advance the Kingdom in their sphere of influence. Sam does a great job explaining the nuances and principles of exercising spiritual power in Christ! The practical aspects are most relevant as the book does not adhere to "pie in the sky" Christianity or popular Spiritual Warfare fads!

So get ready to be educated, empowered and deployed into the war that is raging around us, a war for the souls of humanity! Get ready to take your place in the Army of God for this is why this book is on your hands.

-Greg V Hurd

Preface

We are in a war. There are two opposing sides. One is known as the Kingdom of Light, the other is the domain of darkness. The two sides are incompatible and each has its military.

This book serves as a wartime manual for those in the Kingdom of Light. We are to **"Fight the good fight of the faith."** (1 Timothy 6:12a) To battle effectively, we need to be equipped with tactical understanding and trained in the weaponry at our disposal.

Our enemy has been disarmed. Jesus Christ has triumphed over death, Hell, and the grave. As children of light, through faith in our Lord Jesus, His victory is now ours! The Kingdom of light is stronger than the domain of darkness. This is why the enemy typically does not directly attack soldiers of God. Since the devil and his cohorts have been disarmed, attacking us straight-on would cause them to scatter in different directions as the terrified cowards they are. This is why they strategize asymmetrical schemes.

In the following sections we will expose the enemies' battle plans, gain insight into their tactics, and familiarize ourselves with the victorious arsenal we have as children of the Most High God. In Christ, we are victorious!

-Sam Hager

Psywar
[**sahy**-wawr]

noun

psychological warfare.

adjective

of, relating to, or characteristic of psychological warfare:

to wage a psywar campaign against the enemy.

(Definition of Psywar | Dictionary.com, n.d.)

We are currently engaged in psychological warfare. **"Do not be conformed to this world but be transformed by the renewal of your mind, that by testing you may discern what is the will of God, what is good and acceptable and perfect."** (Romans 12:2)

[1.1 Psychological Warfare]

The enemy deploys psyops against soldiers of God. The forces of darkness seek to distract, deceive, misinform, disinform, discourage, demoralize, confuse, and utterly paralyze soldiers of light. This is one reason 1 Peter 5:8 instructs us to, **"Be sober-minded; be watchful. Your adversary the** devil prowls around like a roaring lion, seeking someone to devour."

It is vital that we stay "sober-minded" in this psywar. The original word translated "sober-minded" is νήφω which is transliterated as népho and is defined as, **"properly, to be sober (not drunk), not intoxicated; (figuratively) free from illusion, i.e. from the intoxicating influences of sin (like the impact of selfish passion, greed, etc.)**

3525 /népho ("be sober, unintoxicated") refers to having *presence of mind* (clear judgment), enabling someone to be *temperate* (self-controlled). 3525 /népho ("uninfluenced by intoxicants") means to have "one's wits (faculties) about them," which is the opposite of being *irrational*." (*Strong's Greek: 3525. νήφω (Néphó) -- to Be Sober, to Abstain from Wine, n.d.*)

The devil searches for soft-targets. Intoxicated people are such targets who expose themselves to the unnecessary risk of becoming prisoners of war. The stakes are high in this psychological warfare. The enemies of God desire to devour their opposition. They want to devour soldiers of light by making them prisoners of war. The goal of the enemy is to surround us in total darkness. This would eliminate our ability to effectively fight them.

We remain harder to devour when we stay unintoxicated, level-headed, and rational. Drunkenness comes in many ways. We can of course become drunk with alcohol, but there are many other things that can intoxicate us such as:

- Drugs
- Passions
- Pride
- Obsessions
- Feelings

This relates to control. There are drugs or medicines that can aid in healing when taken in moderation, but can cause altered states of reality when abused. Being passionate can be good when regulated wisely. Our Commander wants us to operate in self-control. **"But the fruit of the Spirit is love, joy, peace, patience, kindness, goodness, faithfulness, gentleness, self-control; against such things there is no law."** (Galatians 5:22-23)

The domain of darkness engages in various psyops. These are specialized psychological operations using unconventional tactics with the goal of achieving dominance in the psywar battlefield. Make no mistake; Satan and his military strategically plot to steal, kill, and destroy.

A classic psyop example is when a giant named Goliath taunted the army of Israel.

[1.2 Classic Psyop]

"He stood and shouted to the ranks of Israel, "Why have you come out to draw up for battle? Am I not a Philistine, and are you not servants of Saul? Choose a man for yourselves, and let him come down to me. If he is able to fight with me and kill me, then we will be your servants. But if I prevail against him and kill him, then you shall be our servants and serve us." And the Philistine said, "I defy the ranks of Israel this day. Give me a man, that we may fight together." When Saul and all Israel heard these words of the Philistine, they were dismayed and greatly afraid."
(1 Samuel 17:8-11)

This psychological operation used threats. It was designed to demoralize, intimidate, and scare the soldiers of Israel. It temporarily worked. This psyop neutralized God's people for a time. Fear infiltrated their thinking causing them to retreat from the battle.

As we know, David ultimately defeated Goliath. David showed us how we could overcome Goliath's psyop. God was already on Israel's side. What God needed was for someone to believe that truth.

Faith in God is a stronger force than fearing the enemy!

In **2 Timothy 1:7** we read, **"for God gave us a spirit not of fear but of power and love and self-control."** Our Commander has transferred power, love, and self-control from His Spirit into our spirits. The Douay-Rheims 1899 American Edition translation uses the word **"sobriety"** for self-control in this verse. We need to utilize the resources given to us so that we are sober-minded. We need to fully embrace the truth. We need to see reality from the perspective of God. The military of darkness has many agents trying to bring poisons into our bodies and minds. If enemy operatives can pull us away from sobriety and into intoxication, then it will be easier for them to dominate our thinking.

The domain of darkness wages war against God and His people. Jesus identified the devil as, **"the father of lies"** in **John 8:44.** We will expose this further in section 3 **"The Enemy And His Soldiers Of Darkness."**

Forces of darkness strategically scheme against forces of light. Their common weapons include:

- Distortions
- Fabrications

- Falsifications
- Misleadings
- Misrepresentations
- Imposters
- Counterfeits
- Forgeries
- Myths

[1.3 Common Weapons Of Darkness]

The various tactics of the enemy aim to take as much psychological territory as possible. Ultimately the enemy wants to steal, kill, and destroy you. If the domain of darkness can't utterly remove you from the battlefield, they will try to kill your understanding of the truth thereby turning you into a spiritually dead sacrifice. If neither of those objectives can be accomplished, then they will stealthily attempt to take things away from you. Jesus said, **"The thief comes only to steal and kill and destroy. I came that they may have life and have it abundantly."** (John 10:10)

The domain of darkness is weaker in every way than the Kingdom of light. As a royal priest in the Lord's military, you have every type of defensive and offensive weapon to enforce the enemy's defeat. To counteract your dominance, darkness uses deceptive philosophies attempting to disarm you. **"See to it that no one takes you captive by philosophy and empty deceit, according to human tradition, according to the elemental spirits of the world, and not according to Christ."** (Colossians 2:8) Soldiers of darkness deploy seducing reasonings endeavoring to captivate you into captivity. Their objective is to get you to quit fighting them by making you a prisoner of war!

The conversation Jesus had with Pilate highlights how someone can be captivated by philosophy and empty deceit. **"Jesus answered, "My kingdom is not of this world. If my kingdom were of this world, my servants would have been fighting, that I might not be delivered over to the Jews. But my kingdom is not from the world."** (John 18:36) Many things were expressed from Jesus here, but observe Pilate's interactions in the following verses. **"Then Pilate said to him, "So you are a king?" Jesus answered, "You say that I am a king. For this purpose I was born and for this purpose I have come into the world—to bear witness to the truth. Everyone who is of the truth listens to my voice." 38 Pilate said to him, "What is truth? After he had said this, he went back outside to the Jews and told them, "I find no guilt in him.""** (John 18:37-38) Pilate asked the question, **"What is truth?"** while looking at the

7

One Who is truth! Pilate didn't listen for an answer so apparently he did not really desire to know the truth.

Asking questions without wanting answers indicates a mind that already has determined ideas. When a person is taken captive by a godless philosophy, they embrace elaborate concepts that fuel pride. Empty deceit is just that - it's empty! It is void of actual substance, but it deceptively masquerades as real knowledge. The prisoner of war captured by philosophy and empty deceit will be tricked into believing disinformation. If the domain of darkness can convince you to believe their counterintelligence, they will suppress your ability to conquer them. Instead of fighting the good fight of faith, you will either fight the wrong battles or you will not be engaged in the war at all.

When things are "**not according to Christ**" (Colossians 2:8b,) they don't line up with the anointed will of God. Antichrist spirits strive to oppose and replace the truth of Christ. The truth of Christ is reality. Antichrist spirits attempt to usher you into an alternate reality. (For more on "**Alternate Realities**" see section 4.) If you believe their version of the truth, you will be captured!

When the truth is resisted and a counterfeit "truth" is presented, it functions as a veil of blindness. **"And even if our gospel is veiled, it is veiled to those who are perishing. 4 In their case the god of this world has blinded the minds of the unbelievers, to keep them from seeing the light of the gospel of the glory of Christ, who is the image of God."** (2 Corinthians 4:3-4) The commander of darkness does not share the gospel. Satan and his warmongers attack you with propaganda designed to keep you blind to the true reality of Christ.

As we deliberate over the psywar we are currently engaged in, it is fitting to know that the forces of darkness fight against us, but Jesus has already fought for us. The devil tries to obscure the cross because that is where darkness was defeated. Jesus won the battle for us on the cross! **"He canceled the record of the charges against us and took it away by nailing it to the cross. 15 In this way, he disarmed the spiritual rulers and authorities. He shamed them publicly by his victory over them on the cross."** (Colossians 2:14-15 NLT)

Victorious Commander And His Soldiers Of Light

"I am Alpha and Omega, the beginning and the ending, saith the Lord, which is, and which was, and which is to come, the Almighty." (Revelation 1:8 KJV)

Almighty is the Lord! As the Lord's soldiers, we are victorious. We are on the side that has won, is winning, and will win!

[2.1 Victorious]

God is the King above all kings! God is the King and rules the kingdom of light. Satan has a kingdom too, but it is inferior to the kingdom of God in every way! Though Lucifer was originally created by God as a powerful angel, he led a rebellion away from the established reign of Almighty God. We will look more at the character and schemes of the devil in section 3 **"The Enemy And His Soldiers Of Darkness."**

"For the Lord Most High is awesome. He is the great King of all the earth. 3 He subdues the

nations before us, putting our enemies beneath our feet." (Psalm 47:2-3 NLT) There is none higher than our God! He is the great King! We are in a war, but the Lord Most High wins every battle. This is not to say that everyone does what He instructs them to do. **"The Lord is not slow to fulfill his promise as some count slowness, but is patient toward you, not wishing that any should perish, but that all should reach repentance."** (2 Peter 3:9) God wields supremacy as He should but not in the sense that He controls the decisions of people. In His sovereignty, He has decided to give people the ability to decide. Though the Lord desires people to reach the conclusion that they should repent, many refuse. It is not the will of God that prisoners of darkness stay enslaved to the devil, but if they reject the gospel of Jesus, there is no other escape from their condemnation.

People are either condemned in the domain of darkness, or they are free in the Kingdom of the Most High God. **"He has delivered us from the domain of darkness and transferred us to the kingdom of his beloved Son,"** (Colossians 1:13) The power that liberated us was the good news of Jesus Christ. **"For I am not ashamed of the gospel of Christ, for it is the power of God to salvation for everyone who believes, for the Jew first and also for the Greek."** (Romans 1:16 NKJV)

We effectively fight the good fight of faith when we know the objectives of our Commander. He wants to rescue people trapped in darkness. As His warriors, we are to join Him in seeking and saving the lost. We do this by sharing His good news with others.

[2.2 Good News]

We have been transferred from darkness to light by receiving Jesus. We are now able to help others to come out of darkness! The simplest of ways to do this is by proclaiming the gospel of Jesus Christ. The gospel holds the power of God to save people.

"The Lord is a warrior; Yahweh is his name!" (Exodus 15:3 NLT) You cannot take away the warring character from the Lord. He is a warrior! You need to appropriate this revelation from God. **"When Joshua was by Jericho, he lifted up his eyes and looked, and behold, a man was standing before him with his drawn sword in his hand. And Joshua went to him and said to him, "Are you for us, or for our adversaries?" 14 And he said, "No; but I am the commander of the army of the Lord. Now I have come." And Joshua fell on his face to the earth and worshiped and said to him, "What does my lord say to his servant?" 15 And the commander of the Lord's army said to Joshua, "Take off your sandals from your feet, for the place**

where you are standing is holy." And Joshua did so." (Joshua 5:13-15)

God has an army. God is a warrior. He is in command of His angels. One-third of them rebelled against God to follow the devil, but two-thirds remained faithful to their Commander. (Side note: one-third = 33%. The occult likes the number 33.)

It's good to understand angels. They worship God, and they are sent like wind and fire. **"Regarding the angels, he says, "He sends his angels like the winds, his servants like flames of fire."'** (Hebrews 1:7 NLT)

Angels are ministering spirits. They carry out directives from God. They assist believers in Christ and aid in setting up situations for people to hear the gospel. **"And to which of the angels has he ever said, "Sit at my right hand until I make your enemies a footstool for your feet"? 14 Are they not all ministering spirits sent out to serve for the sake of those who are to inherit salvation?"** (Hebrews 1:13-14)

Angels are worshippers and warriors. In that respect we are like them and battle alongside them in spiritual warfare. There is a distinction between angels and humans, but we are on the same side.

Of course, I am referring to the faithful angels that serve the Living God.

"Now war arose in heaven, Michael and his angels fighting against the dragon. And the dragon and his angels fought back, 8 but he was defeated, and there was no longer any place for them in heaven." (Revelation 12:7-8) From this text, we read of a war in heaven between angels of light and angels of darkness. Angels of light prevail as they are on God's side. Although we are not angels, we are in the same kingdom. We need to know that we are destined to rule and reign in Christ Jesus. We do not need to have a pessimistic, defeated mentality. In Christ, we are victorious!

When we hear the gospel of Jesus Christ, spiritual light shines on the spiritual part of us giving us the ability to awaken and arise from the dead. **"for anything that becomes visible is light. Therefore it says, "Awake, O sleeper, and arise from the dead, and Christ will shine on you.""** (Ephesians 5:14) As we receive the light of Christ, we are translated out of darkness and into light. **"giving thanks to the Father, who has qualified you to share in the inheritance of the saints in light. 13 He has delivered us from the domain of darkness and transferred us to the kingdom of his beloved Son, 14 in whom we have**

redemption, the forgiveness of sins."
(Colossians 1:12-14)

Since we are now in the kingdom of the beloved Son of God, we are citizens of light. As citizens of light, we have overcome the power of darkness. **"For everyone who has been born of God overcomes the world. And this is the victory that has overcome the world—our faith."** (1 John 5:4) We did not save ourselves, but we said yes to the salvation of Christ Jesus our Lord. Through faith in Christ, we were reborn into the kingdom of God. In His glorious kingdom, we are no longer subject to the tyranny of darkness. We are free and have been commissioned to be freedom fighters!

We were once enslaved to darkness but are now in the light. We oppose darkness. We are in a conflict against the spiritual forces that are holding people hostage. We fight for hostages held by spiritual forces of evil! **"For we do not wrestle against flesh and blood, but against the rulers, against the authorities, against the cosmic powers over this present darkness, against the spiritual forces of evil in the heavenly places."** (Ephesians 6:12) We are free men and women who worship God and fight the good fight of faith so that prisoners of darkness can be liberated!

In this spiritual battle, we have armor and weaponry. **"Stand therefore, having fastened on the belt of truth, and having put on the breastplate of righteousness, 15 and, as shoes for your feet, having put on the readiness given by the gospel of peace. 16 In all circumstances take up the shield of faith, with which you can extinguish all the flaming darts of the evil one; 17 and take the helmet of salvation, and the sword of the Spirit, which is the word of God,"** (Ephesians 6:14-17)

[2.3 Armor And Weaponry]

"...having fastened the belt of truth..." The truth of Jesus is your security. He is the truth and has prayed to the Father for us to receive the Spirit of truth. As we get into the word of God, which is truth, we are renewed in our minds. This helps us to be sober-minded and ready to defend against the lies of the enemy.

"...having put on the breastplate of righteousness..." We are to wear righteousness as armor. This is the righteousness of Jesus Christ that He transfers to those who place their faith in Him. **"For our sake he made him to be sin who knew no sin, so that in him we might become the righteousness of God."** (2 Corinthians 5:21)

He died for our sins so that we can live in His righteousness. We are made right with God through the blood of Jesus!

"...as shoes for your feet, having put on the readiness given by the gospel of peace..." As soldiers of light, we are to be ready to help prisoners of war defect from the domain of darkness. Everywhere our feet take us is a place for us to share the good news of Jesus. Regardless of customs, policies, laws, or any other type of restriction, we are authorized to proclaim the gospel. The right to do this comes from the One Who wields ultimate authority. **"And Jesus came and said to them, "All authority in heaven and on earth has been given to me. 19 Go therefore and make disciples of all nations, baptizing them in the name of the Father and of the Son and of the Holy Spirit, 20 teaching them to observe all that I have commanded you. And behold, I am with you always, to the end of the age."** (Matthew 28:18-20)

"In all circumstances take up the shield of faith, with which you can extinguish all the flaming darts of the evil one..." Faith is a shield. Have faith in God. Have the faith of God. When the evil one shoots accusation, temptation, confusion, and other types of flaming arrows at you; the faith of God will extinguish them all!

"Now faith is the assurance of things hoped for, the conviction of things not seen."
(Hebrews 11:1) A force-field is created around you when you are convinced of the invisible realities of God. This is your defensive protection that the darts of the evil one will not penetrate. **"But you, beloved, building yourselves up in your most holy faith and praying in the Holy Spirit,"** (Jude 1:20) Be strong in the faith of God!

"...and take the helmet of salvation..." Wear salvation as a helmet. The realization of salvation in Christ protects us against psychological operations the enemy uses against us. When darkness tries to convince us that we are disconnected from God, we refute that lie with certainty that we are saved by the blood of Jesus. We don't wear a helmet of man-made salvation. We wear the helmet of salvation in Christ. Jesus saved us and the enemy cannot take that away!

"...and the sword of the Spirit, which is the word of God," This is our weapon; the word of God. Notice how it is, "the sword of the Spirit." To use the word of God as a skilful warrior, we need to be led by the Spirit of God. We can slash at anything using Bible verses, but if we are doing it in our own strength and carnal reasoning, we will commit "friendly-fire." This will cause us to injure people through misapplications of the word instead of fighting for those enslaved.

To effectively use the word of God in battle, we need to follow the leading of the Holy Spirit.

We are loved by the Father. We are saved by the Son. We are led by the Spirit. As we operate as soldiers of light on the earth, we need to be empowered by the Holy Spirit. Jesus said, **"But you will receive power when the Holy Spirit has come upon you, and you will be my witnesses in Jerusalem and in all Judea and Samaria, and to the end of the earth."** (Acts 1:8) The **"power"** that you receive when the Holy Spirit comes upon you is **"dunamis"** and means **"(miraculous) power, might, strength."** (*Strong's Greek: 1411. δύναμις (Dunamis) -- (Miraculous) Power, Might, Strength, n.d.-b*)

The Enemy And His Soldiers Of Darkness

"And the great dragon was thrown down, that ancient serpent, who is called the devil and Satan, the deceiver of the whole world—he was thrown down to the earth, and his angels were thrown down with him." (Revelation 12:9)

[3.1 The Enemy And His Tactics]

We have an enemy who goes by many names. Here are some:

- Satan
- Lucifer
- The devil
- Dragon
- Deceiver
- Father of lies

"Put on the whole armor of God, that you may be able to stand against the schemes of the devil." (Ephesians 6:11) We need to realize the devil has cunning tactics that he deploys against us. He cannot overpower our will.

He cannot just come in and do whatever he wants to the child of God. Satan uses asymmetrical spiritual warfare strategies against us. He cannot impose his venomous will upon us. So in order to bring destruction into our lives, the devil plots crafty ways to introduce cursed information to us so that we will appropriate it and thereby harm ourselves. Another translation of Ephesians 6:11 puts it this way, **"Put on the full armor of God so that you can stand against the tactics of the Devil."** (HCSB) The devil has tactics, but we have the armor and weaponry of Almighty God!

Lies are weapons wielded by the devil. Satan is the originator of lies as he was identified by Jesus as, **"the father of lies"** in John 8:44. We should not overlook this basic reality. Lies come from Satan. He is the source of deception. His military of darkness will utilize deceptive methods against people in order to confuse and lead them astray.

"And I heard a loud voice in heaven, saying, "Now the salvation and the power and the kingdom of our God and the authority of his Christ have come, for the accuser of our brothers has been thrown down, who accuses them day and night before our God." (Revelation 12:10) Satan hurls accusations against us. He constantly wants to dig up any past mistake or failure and point it out. The devil wants to demoralize and paralyze us so that we are ineffective in fighting against his domain of darkness.

"And they have conquered him by the blood of the Lamb and by the word of their testimony, for they loved not their lives even unto death." (Revelation 12:11) Through the blood of Jesus Christ we are victorious! When the enemy and his minions accuse us of past mistakes, we can confess the truth of our forgiveness! Because we have received Jesus and His precious blood, we are now innocent in the sight of Almighty God. Our Commander has translated us out of darkness and although the accuser may bring up things we did in the dark, God has nailed that to the cross and our sins are dead. **"We know that our old sinful selves were crucified with Christ so that sin might lose its power in our lives. We are no longer slaves to sin."** (Romans 6:6 NLT)

Satan is evil and tempts us. His military is full of fallen angels that try to seduce us into immorality. **"Now the works of the flesh are evident: sexual immorality, impurity, sensuality, 20 idolatry, sorcery, enmity, strife, jealousy, fits of anger, rivalries, dissensions, divisions, 21 envy, drunkenness, orgies, and things like these. I warn you, as I warned you before, that those**

who do such things will not inherit the kingdom of God." (Galatians 5:19-21)

Soldiers of darkness seek to exalt ways that are contrary to God and His ways. **"For all that is in the world—the desires of the flesh and the desires of the eyes and pride of life—is not from the Father but is from the world."** (1 John 2:16)

The word "Lucifer" is found one time in the Bible. It is in Isaiah 14 in a proverb against the king of Babylon. The Hebrew word for Lucifer is transliterated **"helel"** and means **"a shining one."** (*Strong's Hebrew: 1966.* הֵילֵל *(Helel) -- a Shining One*, n.d.) There was a human king of Babylon, but the nature he operated in was not godly. It was satanic. The Old Testament is the New Testament concealed and the New Testament is the Old Testament revealed. Through the lens of our redemption found in our Lord Jesus, we understand mysterious, previously concealed, meanings contained in the scriptures. We look through the revelations of the New Testament as born-again believers in Christ, guided by the Holy Spirit, to accurately understand the Old Testament. Since we now have partaken of the divine nature (see 2 Peter 1:3-4), we can see beyond the natural and into the spiritual!

Lucifer is a fitting name for Satan. **"And no wonder, for even Satan disguises himself as**

24

an angel of light." (2 Corinthians 11:14) This deceiver disguises himself so that you won't easily recognize him. If Satan walked up to you with a pitch-fork, red horns, goat hooves, and a tail then you could easily spot him. That type of imagery is another part of his deception. Sure some people will crave evil so much that they would gladly want such a creature, but Satan wants to have more followers than those who openly embrace satanism. The devil desires others to do his bidding without their awareness. Many say they don't believe in a God or a devil but are exemplifying certain attributes of the satanic nature.

Satan is a deceiver who uses multiple disguises. The snake will morph into a dragon. He led an open rebellion against the true God, but will try to co-opt gatherings of godly people in order to inject any amount of nefarious venom that he can get away with. The father of lies tries to persuade humanity to sympathize with him so that they will despise the true God.

The devil, with his fallen angels, has been working since the beginning to trick humanity. When Adam and Eve fell for the devil's craftiness, they fell too. They exchanged the pure nature they had from God, for the evil nature of Satan. Now we live in a world system largely influenced by satanic disinformation which is contrary to the knowledge of God. **"We know that we are children of God and that the world around us is under the control of the evil one."** (1 John 5:19 NLT) Since we walk in a fallen world, we must rely on the light of God to shine our way. **"Your word is a lamp to my feet and a light to my path."** (Psalm 119:105) Only through wielding the sword of the Spirit properly can we cut through the dark lies of the enemy all around us.

[3.2 Enemy Forces]

The devil has dark spiritual forces working in his kingdom. **"For we do not wrestle against flesh and blood, but against the rulers, against the authorities, against the cosmic powers over this present darkness, against the spiritual forces of evil in the heavenly places."** (Ephesians 6:12) The original word for "rulers" is transliterated "arché" and means "**beginning, origin.**" *Strong's Greek: 746. ἀρχή (arché) -- beginning, origin. (n.d.).* These dark unseen rulers are sources of evil. They are like the roots of the manifested chaos that is seen in the earth. We don't wrestle against the fruit carriers; our fight is against the source of the rotten fruit.

After **"rulers"** we have **"the authorities"** this is **from the Greek word exousia and means, "power to act, authority."** *Strong's Greek: 1849. ἐξουσία (exousia) -- power to act, authority. (n.d.).*

There is a flow of delegated authority in the domain of darkness. Their system is a counterfeit to God's system, so some of the chain of command structure looks similar to the kingdom of light.

Next we see **"the cosmic powers over this present darkness"** which comes from the original word transliterated kosmokratór and means, **"a ruler of this world."** *Strong's Greek: 2888.* *κοσμοκράτωρ (kosmokratór) -- a ruler of this world.* (n.d.). This type of ruler is operating independent from God. This is an invisible enforcer of the enemy's agenda over fallen humanity. Kosmokrators may be unseen with natural eyes, but their effects are not invisible. The actions of rebellious people clearly display the drive of the satanic enforcers of darkness.

Lastly from Ephesians 6:12 we wrestle, **"against the spiritual forces of evil in the heavenly places."** This would cover all other evil spirits that would try to influence us on the earth. What we see is a hierarchy of evil power from the ground troops, up the ranks, all the way up to the commander of the domain of darkness. The good news for soldiers of light is this, Jesus triumphed over them all! Since we not only fight in the light, we ourselves are in the light therefore making us stronger than the entire military of darkness! No matter how dark, no matter how many forces of darkness, no matter if the devil himself comes against us, the Greater One lives in us and we live in Him! We are in the light and darkness cannot overpower the light!

[3.3 Imposters]

There are people who pretend to be who they are not. Imposters stealthily try to infiltrate the gathering of soldiers of light.

"For certain people have crept in unnoticed who long ago were designated for this condemnation, ungodly people, who pervert the grace of our God into sensuality and deny our only Master and Lord, Jesus Christ." (Jude 1:4) In such a short book of the Bible, Jude has a lot to say about spiritual impostors! We see that they are ungodly people. It is interesting to know that there are people who will try to come alongside godly people but will refuse to embrace God.

"For God did not send his Son into the world to condemn the world, but in order that the world might be saved through him. 18 Whoever believes in him is not condemned, but whoever does not believe is condemned already, because he has not believed in the name of the only Son of God." (John 3:17-18) The infiltrators talked about in Jude 1:4, **"who long ago**

were designated for this condemnation" are those who have not believed in the Son of God. They never received the gift of eternal life in Christ, for if they had, they would not still be condemned. Although they could have escaped through Jesus, the Son of God, they remain condemned. This is not what God desires for them, but they choose to stay condemned by not receiving the Lord Jesus Christ.

Through their unregenerate minds, they twist the grace of God. Grace is a gift to be received from God to bring liberty, but there are impostors who, from their flesh-dominated imprisonment, will manufacture an application of "grace" that is a different kind of "liberty." These condemned frauds, who could have escaped condemnation through the pure grace of God, instead transfer grace into casting off moral restraint. Their twisted application of grace makes them feel free to commit all sorts of sexually perverse behavior with no regard for God ordained consequences.

"just as Sodom and Gomorrah and the surrounding cities, which likewise indulged in sexual immorality and pursued unnatural desire, serve as an example by undergoing a punishment of eternal fire. 8 Yet in like manner these people also, relying on their dreams, defile the flesh, reject authority, and blaspheme the glorious ones." (Jude 1:7-8)

Here in the New Testament, we are reminded of the fate of Sodom and Gomorrah and surrounding areas where people indulged in sexual immorality and pursued unnatural desires. The people who try to creep into our gatherings by stealth will be like those of Sodom and Gomorrah. Time and divine discernment are valuable resources to the soldiers of light. Over time, it is easier to see through facades as truth inevitably comes out. Divine discernment can also help us know what we wouldn't otherwise understand.

"Woe to them! For they walked in the way of Cain and abandoned themselves for the sake of gain to Balaam's error and perished in Korah's rebellion." (Jude 1:11) There will be a reckoning. Sowing precedes reaping and without accepting the pure grace of God and escaping their condemnation, they will suffer punishment.

"These are hidden reefs at your love feasts, as they feast with you without fear, shepherds feeding themselves; waterless clouds, swept along by winds; fruitless trees in late autumn, twice dead, uprooted; 13 wild waves of the sea, casting up the foam of their own shame; wandering stars, for whom the gloom of utter darkness has been reserved forever." (Jude 1:12-13) Selfish blemishes without regard for any warning from God are how these impostors are regarded. They will be tossed to and fro with different winds or fads. They may have the appearance of godliness but deny the power of the gospel to actually save them. These people can say many appropriate sounding words as they have gleaned the vocabulary through close proximity, but ultimately they are utterly dead. It is sad for them. May the wandering stars upon the earth now receive the Lord Jesus Christ and escape condemnation before it is forever too late for them!

Alternate Realities

The enemy deploys disinformation campaigns to cause division. The common war tactic is to divide and conquer. The domain of darkness manufactures psyops to create alternate visions of reality. Consider the word division. Take the first part [di] meaning two and then put in [vision] what is seen. Combined you have two different visions. These will naturally compete against each other. Where there is division there is competition for dominance.

[4.1 Division]

"I appeal to you, brothers, to watch out for those who cause divisions and create obstacles contrary to the doctrine that you have been taught; avoid them. 18 For such persons do not serve our Lord Christ, but their own appetites, and by smooth talk and flattery they deceive the hearts of the naive." (Romans 16:17-18) Here we see those causing divisions are creating obstacles which in the original language is *"skándalon." (Strong's Greek: 4625. σκάνδαλον (Skandalon) -- a Stick for Bait (of a Trap), Generally a Snare, a Stumbling Block, an Offense, n.d.)*

Enemies of the cross will use smooth talk and flattery as weapons. They try to gain psychological mastery over their targets by using deceptive compliments. It is okay to use positive words and compliments, but your enemies will mask destructive intentions with applause and adulation. This is another example of asymmetrical spiritual warfare. The enemy camouflages objectives using baiting words.

This should alert us to the need for discernment. Since you can at any time be the target of a psyop, it is important that you possess biblical discernment. **"The wisdom of the prudent is to discern his way, but the folly of fools is deceiving."** (Proverbs 14:8) **"Do not be conformed to this world, but be transformed by the renewal of your mind, that by testing you may discern what is the will of God, what is good and acceptable and perfect."** (Romans 12:2)

The Word of God is reality. Absorbing the Bible supplies us with the perception of God. We look into the spiritual world through God's perspective when we filter our thoughts with His Word. In order to really know what His Word means, we need to rely on the Holy Spirit for divine understanding.

[4.2 Holy Spirit]

Talking with His disciples, Jesus said, **"I still have many things to say to you, but you cannot bear them now. 13 When the Spirit of truth comes, he will guide you into all the truth, for he will not speak on his own authority, but whatever he hears he will speak, and he will declare to you the things that are to come."** (John 16:12-13) The natural disciples didn't have the capacity to handle certain things without the Holy Spirit. Notice how Jesus referred to Him as the "Spirit of truth." The word for truth is "**alétheia**" and in its usage means, "**truth, but not merely truth as spoken; truth of idea, reality, sincerity, truth in the moral sphere, divine truth revealed to man, straightforwardness.**" (*Strong's Greek: 225. ἀλήθεια (Alétheia) -- Truth, n.d.*)

The Holy Spirit is the Spirit of reality! We cannot truly know God's perspective irrespective of the Spirit of truth. We need to be baptized in the Holy Spirit as Jesus said in Acts chapter 1. As soon as you receive Jesus, you can be baptized in the Holy Spirit! When we are born-again, we are born of the Spirit. This positions us to simultaneously or anytime thereafter to be baptized in the Holy Spirit. **"But you will receive power when the Holy Spirit has come upon you, and you will be my witnesses in Jerusalem and in all Judea and Samaria, and to the end of the earth."** (Acts 1:8)

True reality is revealed to us by the Holy Spirit. That is what Jesus said the Holy Spirit would do. The enemy seeks to keep us away from true reality. The military of darkness would like to have us focus on alternate realities. Just as we are to, **"Be sober-minded..."** (1 Peter 5:8a) we are also instructed in Ephesians 5:18 in the KJV, **"And be not drunk with wine, wherein is excess; but be filled with the Spirit;"** Here we see a contrast between drunkenness and Spirit-filled living.

Consider the gifts of the Spirit of God found in 1 Corinthians 12:8-10 from the NKJV, **"for to one is given the word of wisdom through the Spirit, to another the word of knowledge through the same Spirit, 9 to another faith by the same Spirit, to another gifts of healings by the same Spirit, 10 to another the working of miracles, to another prophecy, to another discerning of spirits, to another *different* kinds of tongues, to another the interpretation of tongues."** The Bible repeatedly emphasizes the point that there are many different gifts, each distributed through the Holy Spirit. We need to understand that the domain of darkness tries to keep us from receiving every gift that God wants to give us.

[4.3 Gifts]

The Holy Spirit gives words of wisdom. The enemy gives counterfeit wisdom. A word of wisdom from the Holy Spirit will be life-giving and truly wise. **"For the Lord gives wisdom; from his mouth come knowledge and understanding;"** (Proverbs 2:6) The enemy will give a twisted "word of wisdom." James 3:14-16 declares, **"But if you have bitter jealousy and selfish ambition in your hearts, do not boast and be false to the truth. 15 This is not the wisdom that comes down from above, but is earthly, unspiritual, demonic. 16 For where jealousy and selfish ambition exist, there will be disorder and every vile practice."** So we see there is a godly wisdom and alternative demonic wisdom. To help us discern between the two types of wisdom, the Bible goes on to say in James 3:17, **"But the wisdom from above is first pure, then peaceable, gentle, open to reason, full of mercy and good fruits, impartial and sincere."**

The Holy Spirit gives words of knowledge. These differ from words of wisdom as they may be specific to current events and not tied to divine principles. A word of knowledge may include direct intel on a specific, current plot the enemy has to harm you at a given time. You could receive a word of knowledge concerning an incursion against one of your children.

The enemy has alternate words of knowledge. Soothsaying and divination are some of the ways these counterfeit words come about.

They are deceptive. They are not life-giving, but lead to death. An example of this would be a psychic saying they are in contact with a deceased relative and have knowledge that only your relative would have known. People get tricked by this specific knowledge not realizing that it is coming through a familiar spirit. This would have been a spiritual being in the kingdom of darkness that was familiar with your deceased relative and remembered or documented certain things. From their archives they reenact events impersonating your loved one. This causes many to stray from faith in the life-giving words of the Spirit of God.

The Holy Spirit gives the gift of faith. The enemy tempts us with a fake faith. Instead of trusting in God and His goodness, the enemy wants us to believe anything else. One main seduction of the kingdom of darkness is to entice you to believe that you do not need God. This comes through a variety of ways. Fear is a weapon of choice in the enemy's camp. Operating in fear is antithetical to faith. Through faith in God, through the faith of God, you can speak to the mountains and watch as they are cast into the sea. Through fear you will speak of the overwhelming circumstances against you and be swallowed up in hopelessness. Warrior of God, don't be intimidated by fear. Have faith in Almighty God! **"There is no fear in love, but perfect love casts out fear. For fear has to do**

with punishment, and whoever fears has not been perfected in love." (1 John 4:18)

Gifts of healing come through the Holy Spirit. Alternate healings come through the enemy. The enemy may mask the pain temporarily while natural healing occurs and then take credit for the healing. The enemy also may have some type of healing medication that carries another time-released problem that will need more medication in the future. Witch doctors concoct all sorts of evil things to trick you, but their power is from darkness and will not give you lasting relief.

God desires for you to be healthy and whole. The enemy desires to make you sick and dependent on sources that promise relief other than God. There are good doctors who want to help, but there are also bad doctors who want money above all else. In your natural dealings ask God to help you find good doctors if needed. **"Beloved, I pray that you may prosper in all things and be in health, just as your soul prospers."** (3 John 1:2)

By the way, gifts are unearned. Notice how the Holy Spirit likes to give many gifts which are not based on what we do to qualify for them? God is good!

The working of miracles is another gift from the Holy Spirit. Sorcery attempts to produce miracles.

There are examples of certain types of manifestations of alternate miracles in the Bible. In Exodus 7:10-11 from the NKJV we see, **"So Moses and Aaron went in to Pharaoh, and they did so, just as the Lord commanded. And Aaron cast down his rod before Pharaoh and before his servants, and it became a serpent. 11 But Pharaoh also called the wise men and the sorcerers; so the magicians of Egypt, they also did in like manner with their enchantments. 12 For every man threw down his rod, and they became serpents. But Aaron's rod swallowed up their rods."** It is good to note that although the godless performed what appeared to be miraculous signs through their occultic arts, Aaron's rod still swallowed up their rods. We need to understand that the power of God is greater than the power of the enemy. As soldiers in the Lord's military, we have more power than the enforcers of darkness!

Jesus demonstrated a gift of miracles in Matthew 8:24-26, **"And behold, there arose a great storm on the sea, so that the boat was being swamped by the waves; but he was asleep. 25 And they went and woke him, saying, "Save us, Lord; we are perishing." 26 And he said to them, "Why are you afraid, O you of little faith?" Then he rose and rebuked the winds and the sea, and there was a great calm."** You may say, "well, that was Jesus we couldn't do that!"

Hear what Jesus Himself said in John 14:12, **"Truly, truly, I say to you, whoever believes in me will also do the works that I do; and greater works than these will he do, because I am going to the Father."**

The Holy Spirit gives the gift of prophecy. 1 Corinthians 14:3 says, **"On the other hand, the one who prophesies speaks to people for their upbuilding and encouragement and consolation."** We see that God gives this gift of prophecy to bring consolation and encouragement. The word **"upbuilding"** is translated **"strengthens"** in the NLT and **"strengthening"** in the CSB. The enemy has replacements for all of these gifts. The demonic realm will want you to be strengthened in darkness, emboldened to do evil, and consoled by some form of deviancy. In other words, the enemy desires you to be comforted in an arm of a seductress, infused with pride, and become fortified in lies.

Hopefully the contrast is quite clear. The Holy Spirit is a life-giver. The devil is a life-taker.

The Holy Spirit gives the gift called discerning of spirits. Through this divine revelation, we understand whether a spirit is coming from the Kingdom of God or the domain of darkness. This is a holy gift making us sensitive to the spiritual world and where the origination of the words and ideas are coming from.

A knock-off the enemy peddles is occultism. Members of secret societies tend to aspire to rise the ranks/levels/degrees to learn hidden knowledge that is supposedly unattainable to profane outsiders. (We will look more into this in section 5.3 **"Secret Societies."**)

The Holy Spirit gives the gift of tongues. What a beautiful gift it is! 1 Corinthians 14:4a says, **"The one who speaks in a tongue builds up himself..."** There is a divine strength that comes through this gift. Speaking in tongues gives your spirit the ability to pray mysteries and give God thanks!

When people give themselves over to satanic rituals and séances they are engaging in counterfeits of the gift of tongues and the interpretation of tongues. They are attempting to contact spirits and gain insights that are not from God. They will do all sorts of evil things giving homage and allegiance to Satan and other evil spirits.

The Holy Spirit gives the gift of interpretation of tongues which, combined with the gift of tongues, operates essentially like prophecy. This gift will strengthen, encourage, and comfort people.

In this war we are in, it is great that God gives us supernatural gifts so that we can be strong and courageous! God is good!

It is fitting to know that the enemy attempts to entice us into intoxication so as to keep us away from reality. Soldiers of darkness want to blind us to truth by keeping us enraptured in fantasies.

[4.4 Fantasies]

Drug addictions and unhealthy obsessions both want to dominate your thinking. The highs of mind-altering drugs feel good for a time. Obsessing over a particular celebrity or video-game can seem meaningful. These things ultimately fall short of producing lasting peace.

Drugs that call our names over and over, as we submit to them, bring us into imprisonment. **"Do not look at wine when it is red, when it sparkles in the cup and goes down smoothly. 32 In the end it bites like a serpent and stings like an adder. 33 Your eyes will see strange things, and your heart utter perverse things. 34 You will be like one who lies down in the midst of the sea, like one who lies on the top of a mast. 35 "They struck me," you will say, "but I was not hurt; they beat me, but I did not feel it. When shall I awake? I must have another drink."** (Proverbs 23:31-35)

We can be freed and stay free from drug addiction through the power of the Holy Spirit!

It is okay to continually think about God. **"You keep him in perfect peace whose mind is stayed on you, because he trusts in you."** (Isaiah 26:3) It is not okay to push God away to obsess continually over someone or something else. **"You shall have no other gods before me."** (Exodus 20:3) If we find ourselves in idolatry, we need to repent. We need to return to our first love!

Living in a secret world of fantasy is an alternative to residing in the secret place. God wants to spend personal, quality time with us in the secret place. The enemy wants us to spend time in vain imaginations. **"He that dwelleth in the secret place of the most High shall abide under the shadow of the Almighty. 2 I will say of the LORD, He is my refuge and my fortress: my God; in him will I trust."** (Psalm 91:1-2 KJV)

The 5th Column

Weaker enemies oftentimes strategize ways to infiltrate those they seek to defeat. Since overpowering their enemies through brute force is not feasible, tactics of subversion are deployed. The military of darkness is inferior to the Kingdom of light. As a soldier of light in Christ, you are superior over the darkness in every way!

[5.1 Infiltration]

Paul brought these corrective words to the church at Corinth, **"for you are still of the flesh. For while there is jealousy and strife among you, are you not of the flesh and behaving only in a human way?"** (1 Corinthians 3:3) Behaving only in a human way is beneath you if you are born again. Any lost person can be jealous of others, but God has made His people become partakers of the divine nature. We should no longer operate in strife out of our former fallen natures.

We can sabotage the desired goals of God by causing dissensions and forming unnecessary factions. Soldiers of God need to resist the gravitational pull of fallen flesh that tries to drag us into complaints against godly leadership. Jesus gave a leadership structure to the church as gifts.

God wants you to have a heavenly system to grow into maturity in Christ!

"So Christ himself gave the apostles, the prophets, the evangelists, the pastors and teachers, 12 to equip his people for works of service, so that the body of Christ may be built up 13 until we all reach unity in the faith and in the knowledge of the Son of God and become mature, attaining to the whole measure of the fullness of Christ." (Ephesians 4:11-13 NLT)

The enemy cannot withstand the unified church that is flowing in the power of God! **"And I tell you, you are Peter, and on this rock I will build my church, and the gates of hell shall not prevail against it."** (Matthew 16:18) Soldiers of darkness try to infiltrate gatherings of believers so as to tear it down from within. If the enemy can plant seeds of disrespect against church leadership and they take root within enough hearts, bitterness can spring up choking out the flow of raw heavenly power from heaven into everyone involved.

"If anyone teaches a different doctrine and does not agree with the sound words of our Lord Jesus Christ and the teaching that accords with godliness, 4 he is puffed up with conceit and understands nothing. He has an unhealthy craving for controversy and for quarrels about words, which produce envy,

dissension, slander, evil suspicions, 5 and constant friction among people who are depraved in mind and deprived of the truth, imagining that godliness is a means of gain." (1 Timothy 6:3-5)

[5.2 Sages, Sorcerers, Magicians]

There are people who are looked to as experts. Those needing help with certain issues want information from people who are knowledgeable of those issues. The 5th column of a government can be corrupted by people who derive their expertise from spiritual darkness.

"So Moses and Aaron went to Pharaoh and did just as the Lord commanded. Aaron cast down his staff before Pharaoh and his servants, and it became a serpent. 11 Then Pharaoh summoned the wise men and the sorcerers, and they, the magicians of Egypt, also did the same by their secret arts. 12 For each man cast down his staff, and they became serpents. But Aaron's staff swallowed up their staffs." (Exodus 7:10-12)

Pharaoh was the leader of Egypt. He had sages, sorcerers, and magicians close to him. Apparently they were his top advisors. They were the experts who supposedly gave wise counsel. What needs to be understood is that there are two sources of wisdom. One source of wisdom is true and is from God. **"For the Lord gives wisdom; from his mouth comes knowledge and understanding;"** (Proverbs 2:6) The other source of wisdom is a counterfeit and comes from the domain of darkness. **"But if you have bitter jealousy and selfish ambition in your hearts, do not boast and be false to the truth. 15 This is not the wisdom that comes down from above, but is earthly, unspiritual, demonic."** (James 3:14-15)

The **"wise men"** in Exodus 7:11 were experts in demonic wisdom. These sages or experts would sound knowledgeable. Their information was not spiritually alive. It may have sounded right, but it would end up leading people down wrong paths. These experts at best would give worthless instructions, at worst they would give advice leading to death.

The "sorcerers" practiced occultic secretive arts. It should be recognized that the free flow of these types of arts are exchanged within fraternal organizations, cults, and secret societies today. Sorcery has to do with practicing witchcraft and casting spells. Also it should be noted that the word "sorcery" is found in Galatians 5:20 and Revelation 18:23 and both times it comes from the original word transliterated, **"pharmakeia"** and means, **"the use of medicine, drugs or spells."** *Strong's Greek: 5331. φαρμακεία (pharmakeia) --*

the use of medicine, drugs or spells. (n.d.)
Biblehub.com.
https://biblehub.com/greek/5331.htm.
It is where we get our modern word for pharmacy.
Although medicines can be used for good, we do
not need to be ignorant that they can very much
be used for sorcery!

 The **"magicians of Egypt"** were well versed in
secret, godless knowledge. They wrote and studied
materials of darkness. Magicians of Egypt would
write and study unholy teachings full of demonic
wisdom. We also understand that magicians
practice trickery.

[5.3 Secret Societies]

**"And he brought me to the entrance of the
court, and when I looked, behold, there was a
hole in the wall. 8 Then he said to me, "Son of
man, dig in the wall." So I dug in the wall, and
behold, there was an entrance."** (Ezekiel 8:7-8)

Secret societies have been around since before
Jesus was born of the virgin Mary! People join
them for various reasons. Oftentimes people will
join secret societies or fraternal organizations for
networking purposes. God did not approve of the
secret society we read about in Ezekiel 8.

"And he said to me, "Go in, and see the vile abominations that they are committing here." 10 So I went in and saw. And there, engraved on the wall all around, was every form of creeping things and loathsome beasts, and all the idols of the house of Israel. 11 And before them stood seventy men of the elders of the house of Israel, with Jaazaniah the son of Shaphan standing among them. Each had his censer in his hand, and the smoke of the cloud of incense went up. 12 Then he said to me, "Son of man, have you seen what the elders of the house of Israel are doing in the dark, each in his room of pictures? For they say, 'The Lord does not see us, the Lord has forsaken the land.'" (Ezekiel 8:9-12)

What these leaders were doing in secret was considered vile and abominable to God. Out of public view, there were walls carved with imagery they would not display in the open. They also engaged in a hidden spirituality. These particular elders were not worshiping the true and living God. Actually, in their room of pictures, they deceived themselves by saying the Lord didn't see them! These people, who were committed to each other in secrecy, were the same who would go out publicly and pretend to worship God. This secluded system produced hypocrisy, idolatry, and a distorted view of the real God.

We need to understand that Jesus did not design a system in which His people would operate in secrecy. On the contrary, Jesus said to us, **"You are the light of the world. A city set on a hill cannot be hidden. 15 Nor do people light a lamp and put it under a basket, but on a stand, and it gives light to all in the house. 16 In the same way, let your light shine before others, so that they may see your good works and give glory to your Father who is in heaven."** (Matthew 5:14-16)

Understand that spiritual leaders would commit vile acts of depraved worship in darkness, but then in public put on a show that looked like they honored the true God above all else. Their secret society gave them what they felt was a safe place from scrutiny so that they could practice occultic behavior without being publicly criticized. The same happens today. People will live by one set of rules and oaths in darkness with their brotherhood (or sisterhood), but try to act normal in the light.

Soldiers of light need to be aware that infiltrators will come out of secret societies, cults, and fraternal organizations desiring to blend in. They will have secretly sworn oaths to others that you don't know about, but will masquerade as people who have an allegiance with light. This is another reason why it is important to have the gift of discerning of spirits in operation today!

Concealed behind esoteric walls of confidentiality many things take place. Two-tiered justice systems are established due to the oaths to protect others within the group regardless of consequences to outsiders. Words are contorted to weave in different meanings. Code words, allegories, symbols, specialized handshakes and other such things are used to help those within the group communicate stealthily with each other. Dealings are crafted outside of the investigative prowess of outsiders. These all create time and space for reckless, immoral, and illegal activity to be devised, executed, and covered up.

It should be noted that not everyone who joins a secretive group does so for a bad reason. Also since there are degrees and levels one progresses through in these mystical sects, people don't get all the information at the beginning. This is by design. Some may not know how bad their clandestine group is, especially in the lower degrees and ranks. Having said that though, it is wise to get out of secret societies and stay away from them. If you are in one, do not disregard this message. Ask the Lord Jesus Christ personally what He would have you do. Settle for nothing less than the King of king's advice on this matter!

If you are unsure whether the society, foundation, collective body, fraternity, order, or group you are in is bad, simply put it to the biblical test.

"**Beloved, do not believe every spirit, but test the spirits to see whether they are from God, for many false prophets have gone out into the world.**" (1 John 4:1) Here are some logical questions to ask yourself:

• Does the group I am in proclaim that Jesus is Lord? "**Therefore I want you to understand that no one speaking in the Spirit of God ever says "Jesus is accursed!" and no one can say "Jesus is Lord" except in the Holy Spirit.**" (1 Corinthians 12:3)

• Does the group tell me to deviate from biblical teaching? "**No wisdom, no understanding, no counsel can avail against the LORD.**" (Proverbs 21:30)

• Am I required to do unbiblical things like swear secret oaths to others in the group? "**But I say to you, Do not take an oath at all, either by heaven, for it is the throne of God,**" (Matthew 5:34)

• Am I obligated to do unbiblical things like lie for my fellow members? "**Do not lie to one another, seeing that you have put off the old self with its practices**" (Colossians 3:9)

• Am I expected to not share that Jesus is the only way to God? "**Jesus said to him, "I am the way, and the truth, and the life. No one comes to the Father except through me.**" (John 14:6)

• Are there rituals, prayers, or other worshipful acts I am to do alongside others who do not believe that Jesus is the Son of God? **"Do not be unequally yoked with unbelievers. For what partnership has righteousness with lawlessness? Or what fellowship has light with darkness? What accord has Christ with Belial? Or what portion does a believer share with an unbeliever?"** (2 Corinthians 6:14-15)

If one or more of the above questions opens up concern about a group you may be in, it is wise to seek the Lord on how to remove yourself from that group. A former 32nd degree Mason has a free resource entitled, "Sample Letter to Demit from Masonic Lodge or similar bodies" on the website https://www.withoneaccord.org/Free-Resources_ep_41.html. This is a tool to help separate from a lodge or group that you biblically identify as being harmful to your walk with God. **"For what does it profit a man to gain the whole world and forfeit his soul?"** (Mark 8:36)

[5.4 Sarx]

Since in Christ you are stronger than hell's military, they attempt to pull you down from within. They cannot impose their will on you, so they try to get you to sabotage yourself. Some common campaigns of the enemy to get your focus off of Jesus include:
- Lust
- Selfishness

- Legalism

"**For all that is in the world—the desires of the flesh and the desires of the eyes and pride of life—is not from the Father but is from the world.**" (1 John 2:16) The Greek word "flesh" in 1 John 2:16 is transliterated "sarx" and generally means the carnal nature of humanity that is not transformed by God. Our physical bodies are not bad. As King David sang, "**I praise you, for I am fearfully and wonderfully made. Wonderful are your works; my soul knows it very well.**" **(Psalm 139:14)** The negative aspect of sarx has to do with self-centeredness.

The world system that is not submitted to God is by default submissive to the devil. A natural person may not actively seek to bend a knee to Satan, but would likely gravitate towards selfishness. The unseen forces of darkness tempt people to gratify their own egos through any and every ungodly means.

Legalism is highly deceptive. It appears to give a person a form of godliness, but denies the power of God. "**O foolish Galatians! Who has bewitched you? It was before your eyes that Jesus Christ was publicly portrayed as crucified. 2 Let me ask you only this: Did you receive the Spirit by works of the law or by hearing with faith? 3 Are you so foolish? Having begun by the Spirit, are**

you now being perfected by the flesh?"
(Galatians 3:1-3) To the Christians in Galatia, the Apostle Paul gave a severe rebuke about their attempts to live godly through carnal efforts.

Apparently someone came into the Galatian assemblies of believers with a bewitching doctrine that took the focus off of the redemptive work of Jesus Christ and put the focus onto the individual's performance. Pursuing spiritual maturity through self effort is foolishness. One cannot overcome the negative aspects of the fallen nature by using the fallen nature! **"But I say, walk by the Spirit, and you will not gratify the desires of the flesh."** (Galatians 5:16)

It's important to note that fighting the flesh with the flesh is unproductive. The way to overcome the lust of the flesh is not to strive to do better or pick yourself up by your own bootstraps. Instead of drawing strength from self-determination, you can simply walk in the Spirit of God. This fellowship and reliance on the Holy Spirit gives us the divine strength to rise above the gravitational pull towards sin. **"*There is* therefore now no condemnation to those who are in Christ Jesus, who do not walk according to the flesh, but according to the Spirit."** (Romans 8:1 NKJV)

More Than Conquerors

How would you engage in psychological warfare if you knew your side had already won? The good news is that Jesus won! When you call on Jesus to save you, He does just that! When you are translated out of the domain of darkness and into the Kingdom of God's dear Son, you enter a place of victory!

[6.1 Victory In Jesus]

"But Mary stood outside by the tomb weeping, and as she wept she stooped down *and looked* into the tomb. 12 And she saw two angels in white sitting, one at the head and the other at the feet, where the body of Jesus had lain. 13 Then they said to her, "Woman, why are you weeping?" She said to them, "Because they have taken away my Lord, and I do not know where they have laid Him." 14 Now when she had said this, she turned around and saw Jesus standing *there,* and did not know that it was Jesus. 15 Jesus said to her, "Woman, why are you weeping? Whom are you seeking?" She, supposing Him to be the gardener, said to Him, "Sir, if You have carried Him away, tell me where You have laid Him, and I will take Him away." 16 Jesus said to her, "Mary!" She turned and said to Him, "Rabboni!" (which is to say, Teacher)." (John 20:11-16 NKJV)

What would you do on the battlefield if you knew your enemy had no weapon that could penetrate the armor you were given? The victory of Jesus is now ours! **"Jesus said to her, "Do not cling to Me, for I have not yet ascended to My Father; but go to My brethren and say to them, 'I am ascending to My Father and your Father, and *to* My God and your God.'"** (John 20:17 NKJV) The risen Lord Jesus wants you to know that His death, burial, and resurrection opened the way for you to have God as your Father. This is good news!

What would you do if enemy combatants could defect to our victorious side? The fallen unseen spiritual forces are beyond our reach to bring over to our side as their fate is sealed. **"For God did not spare even the angels who sinned. He threw them into hell, in gloomy pits of darkness, where they are being held until the day of judgment."** (2 Peter 2:4) While living on the earth, fellow human beings who are hostile to the Kingdom of light are not beyond hope! **"But I say to you, Love your enemies and pray for those who persecute you,"** (Matthew 5:44)

Where would you go if you knew you had the keys to set prisoners of war free? "**And he said to them, "Go into all the world and proclaim the gospel to the whole creation. Whoever believes and is baptized will be saved, but whoever does not believe will be condemned. And these signs will accompany those who believe: in my name they will cast out demons; they will speak in new tongues; they will pick up serpents with their hands; and if they drink any deadly poison, it will not hurt them; they will lay their hands on the sick, and they will recover."'** (Mark 16:15-18)

As a soldier of Christ, you do have the keys that can set the captives free! You can help liberate other people by sharing the good news of Jesus Christ. The same message that you believed that brought you out of darkness, is the same message that others need to hear so they can choose the freedom of Jesus. **"For "everyone who calls on the name of the Lord will be saved." 14 How then will they call on him in whom they have not believed? And how are they to believe in him of whom they have never heard? And how are they to hear without someone preaching?"** (Romans 10:13-14) You do not need to be a preacher at a church to help someone call on the Lord. You can simply tell people what Jesus has done for you. Let them know how you received the Lord Jesus. Tell them Who He is to you now and then ask if they would like Jesus to save them. When they say yes to the gospel and believe in the Lord Jesus, they are saved from darkness and brought into the Kingdom of light!

[6.2 Victory Now]

As a soldier in the Kingdom of God, you are victorious now! You entered into victory when you believed in the Victorious One! Jesus conquered death, hell, and the grave. He is risen! His triumph over death is now available to us. As we believe we are translated into a Kingdom of victory.

Ephesians 1:3 says, **"Blessed be the God and Father of our Lord Jesus Christ, who has blessed us in Christ with every spiritual blessing in the heavenly places,"** We need to embrace the reality that in Christ we have been blessed with every spiritual blessing! Then in Ephesians 1:18-20, the Bible shares, **"having the eyes of your hearts enlightened, that you may know what is the hope to which he has called you, what are the riches of his glorious inheritance in the saints, 19 and what is the immeasurable greatness of his power toward us who believe, according to the working of his great might 20 that he worked in Christ when he raised him from the dead and seated him at his right hand in the heavenly places,"** May you be enlightened to know what you already have in Christ!

"But thanks be to God, who gives us the victory through our Lord Jesus Christ." (1 Corinthians 15:57) We have been translated into the supreme Kingdom by the Almighty King and He has given us His victorious nature! Although we were dead in darkness, now we are alive in the light. Although we were once enemies of God, now we are His beloved children. We are victorious in Christ!

[6.3 Inseparable]

Jesus wants us to understand our union with God. In John 17:21 He prayed, **"that they may all be one, just as you, Father, are in me, and I in you, that they also may be in us, so that the world may believe that you have sent me."** The Apostle Paul elaborated on our connection to the Creator by saying, **"But he who is joined to the Lord becomes one spirit with him."** (1 Corinthians 6:17) With this awareness we understand the answer to the question posed in Romans 8:35 which asks, **"Who shall separate us from the love of Christ? Shall tribulation, or distress, or persecution, or famine, or nakedness, or danger, or sword?"** The obvious conclusion is that nothing shall separate us for nothing is able to overpower God. It is interesting that, after the question asking who could separate us from the love of Christ, many of life's worst problems are listed. They are listed to let us know that if we find ourselves in any or all of these circumstances, we are never unloved by God; not even for a fraction of a second. The love of God is everlasting. His love lasts forever. Like the bones in the legs of Jesus on the cross, the love of Christ is unbroken!

"36 As it is written, "For your sake we are being killed all the day long; we are regarded as sheep to be slaughtered." (Romans 8:36) Here we find that even in death we are loved by God. The kingdom of darkness may just want us dead, but our Father in Heaven never stops cherishing us! Realize that the presence of problems does not equal the absence of love. Even when contempt from the fallen world attacks you without cause, you are continually loved by God.

Jesus said something interesting about the ruler of the fallen world. **"I will no longer talk much with you, for the ruler of this world is coming, and he has nothing in Me."** (John 14:30 NKJV) The ruler of darkness has nothing in Jesus. This is another reason why nothing can separate you from the love of Christ. There is no amount of darkness that can get inside of the light of God. If you are born again, nothing contrary to God can get to the place where His Spirit is connected to your spirit. In Christ you are joined to the Lord, and no devil destined for hell can disconnect your union with the Risen King!

"Keep your life free from love of money, and be content with what you have, for he has said, "I will never leave you nor forsake you."" (Hebrews 13:5) If the enemy can entice you into the love of money, he will get you to look for other sources of provision other than God. If the army of the serpent can get you to become discontent with what you have, it will be easy for them to tempt you into indulging in what God forbids. Keeping your focus on Jesus and His great love for you will help nullify the temptations that are trying to get you to receive "solutions" from the enemy.

Jesus promises to be with us while we are here. When we pass on from this world, Jesus promises that we will be with Him. The abiding presence of God is a beautiful reality for believers in Christ!

[6.4 HYPÉR NIKÁŌ]

"No, in all these things we are more than conquerors through him who loved us."

(Romans 8:37) It doesn't matter what problems we face here on the battlefield, we are more than conquerors through Jesus Christ! God loves us and nothing can take that away!

In Romans 8:37 the phrase, **"more than conquerors"** comes from the compound word in Greek, **"hupernikaó"** which is pronounced, **"hoop-er-nik-ah'-o."** The first word in this compound is transliterated, **"hypér"** and according to *Thayer's Greek-English Lexicon of the New Testament* it means:

I.   **in behalf of, for the sake of**
II.   **over, beyond, more than**
III.   **more, beyond, over**

(Strong's #5228 - ὑπέρ - Old & New Testament Greek Lexical Dictionary. (n.d.). StudyLight.org.)

"Hypér" is the word **"above"** in Philippians 2:9 which says, **"Therefore God has highly exalted him and bestowed on him the name that is above every name,"** Just like we know that the name of Jesus is far above every other name, we need to understand that because we belong to Jesus, we are far above every problem of this life!

The second part of the compound word **"hupernikaó"** is **"nikaó"** and means, **"to *subdue***

(literally or figuratively): - conquer, overcome, prevail, get the victory." (*Strong's #3528 - νικάω - Old & New Testament Greek Lexical Dictionary.* (n.d.). StudyLight.org.)

"**Nikaó**" is the word "**overcomes**" in Luke 11:21-22 which says, "**When a strong man, fully armed, guards his own palace, his goods are safe; 22 but when one stronger than he attacks him and overcomes him, he takes away his armor in which he trusted and divides his spoil.**" Just like the stronger one overcomes the weaker one, God reveals that we overcome the attacks of the enemy, "**through him who loved us.**"

Combining "**hypér**" together with "**nikaó**" reveals our overwhelmingly victorious position in Christ. Because of the victory Jesus won for us on the cross, we live at a level so far above the schemes of the devil. We don't just barely win, we absolutely crush the enemy! Actually, God Himself will crush Satan underneath our feet! "**The God of peace will soon crush Satan under your feet. The grace of our Lord Jesus Christ be with you.**" (Romans 16:20)

The Father's Heart

The Commander of Heaven's Army is also a great Father! The One Who forever reigns supreme is the same Who loves us with an everlasting love. He brings the plans of the enemy to nothing as He draws people to Himself through His Son Jesus the Christ.

[7.1 For God So Loved The World]

After Adam and Eve ate the forbidden fruit, God went to see them and the two hid. God went to where they could hear Him and said to Adam, **"Where are you?"** (Genesis 3:9b) It should be obvious that God knew where they were, but what may not be as obvious is the emotional state of God. The Creator loves, can be grieved, gets angry, rejoices, can be jealous, and experiences every feeling that He gave us. God handles His emotions perfectly as He loves us fully.

Just as He loves us to the highest level, He also hates what is evil to the greatest degree. In Revelation 19:11-12 the Bible records, **"Then I saw heaven opened, and behold, a white horse!**

The one sitting on it is called Faithful and True, and in righteousness he judges and makes war. 12 His eyes are like a flame of fire, and on his head are many diadems, and he has a name written that no one knows but himself." Here we see Jesus the King above all preparing to utterly crush His enemies! "He is clothed in a robe dipped in blood, and the name by which he is called is The Word of God. 14 And the armies of heaven, arrayed in fine linen, white and pure, were following him on white horses. 15 From his mouth comes a sharp sword with which to strike down the nations, and he will rule them with a rod of iron. He will tread the winepress of the fury of the wrath of God the Almighty. 16 On his robe and on his thigh he has a name written, King of kings and Lord of lords." (Revelation 19:13-16)

The Almighty has fury and wrath and will pour it out on His enemies. This is destined to be and nothing will stop it! This is justice. "Then I saw an angel standing in the sun, and with a loud voice he called to all the birds that fly directly overhead, "Come, gather for the great supper of God, 18 to eat the flesh of kings, the flesh of captains, the flesh of mighty men, the flesh of horses and their riders, and the flesh of all men, both free and slave, both small and great."" (Revelation 19:17-18) The great supper of God doesn't get preached about as much as the marriage supper of the Lamb, but they are both realities found in Revelation chapter 19.

"And I saw the beast and the kings of the earth with their armies gathered to make war against him who was sitting on the horse and against his army." (Revelation 19:19) Those who are committed to evil in this end-time war will come against the King of kings. They are unrepentant and do not want the Father or His Son. They are committed to drunkenness, uncleanliness, sexual immorality, lies, sorcery, and every form of wickedness. They are haters of God and have chosen to worship the beast. **"And the beast was captured, and with it the false prophet who in its presence had done the signs by which he deceived those who had received the mark of the beast and those who worshiped its image. These two were thrown alive into the lake of fire that burns with sulfur. 21 And the rest were slain by the sword that came from the mouth of him who was sitting on the horse, and all the birds were gorged with their flesh."** (Revelation 19:20-21) Justice is required for evil. Hell is real.

Going back to when Adam responded to God in Genesis 3:10 we read, **"And he said, "I heard the sound of you in the garden, and I was afraid, because I was naked, and I hid myself.""** Being afraid was brand new to Adam. He never once had the need to fear before he sinned against God. Fear overtook Adam because he had been in a sense born-again, but not how we understand being born-again today. Adam was originally born perfectly, but when he rebelled against God, he was reborn from life into spiritual death. Adam's new spiritually dead nature immediately panicked when God approached. Shame and fear rushed into the mind of Adam causing him to flee from his Creator.

In Genesis 3:11b God asked, **"Who told you that you were naked? Have you eaten of the tree of which I commanded you not to eat?"** Notice that Adam responds by shifting the blame to both Eve and God in the next verse, **"The man said, "The woman whom you gave to be with me, she gave me fruit of the tree, and I ate."** The fallen nature is clearly seen in blame-shifting. Adam who had been full of the life of God, fell into the death of the devil.

"Then the Lord God said to the woman, "What is this that you have done?" The woman said, "The serpent deceived me, and I ate." (Genesis 3:13) The heart of the Father was broken by the fall of the people He loved. **"What is this that you have done?"** Adam and Eve lived in paradise; they had every provision, every pure pleasure in perfection. The two enjoyed a vibrant relationship with their loving Father. They had the life of God, but threw it away for the nature of the serpent.

"So the Lord God said to the serpent:

"Because you have done this,
You *are* cursed more than all cattle,
And more than every beast of the field;
On your belly you shall go,
And you shall eat dust
All the days of your life.

15

And I will put enmity
Between you and the woman,
And between your seed and her Seed;
He shall bruise your head,
And you shall bruise His heel."'

(Genesis 3:14-15 NKJV)

Within God's judgment upon the serpent, He embedded the mysterious two words, **"her Seed."** Previously veiled from understanding, these words from God declared a plan that would unfold throughout generations to make a way for fallen humanity to be reborn, out of death and into the life of God. When God said, **"her Seed"** He proclaimed that the overruling of spiritual death, that had been brought into the world through a deceived woman and consenting man, would come through a consenting woman who God would

71

choose to bring forth His Son into the world! **"Therefore the Lord himself will give you a sign. Behold, the virgin shall conceive and bear a son, and shall call his name Immanuel."** (Isaiah 7:14)

[7.2 That He Gave His Only Begotten Son]

The warring nature of our Father in Heaven should bring a sense of awe. He fights for us and against our enemies. **"For it pleased *the Father that* in Him all the fullness should dwell, 20 and by Him to reconcile all things to Himself, by Him, whether things on earth or things in heaven, having made peace through the blood of His cross."** (Colossians 1:19-20 NKJV) Even though we ourselves were enemies of God, He provided a way for us to defect from the kingdom of darkness. Through the blood of His cross we are brought into the Kingdom of the Son of His love! **"And you, who once were alienated and enemies in your mind by wicked works, yet now He has reconciled 22 in the body of His flesh through death, to present you holy, and blameless, and above reproach in His sight—"** (Colossians 1:21-22 NKJV)

You need to see yourself the way God sees you because viewing yourself any other way is unbiblical and ultimately harmful. You are above reproach in the sight of the Father. It is so magnificent that God would even open a way for you to leave your imprisonment in darkness after willingly participating in warring against Him! If mere freedom was all He provided that would be enough to celebrate forever, but through the blood of Jesus, He also received you into His majestic Kingdom as a blameless citizen! The Father's heart is full of compassion and love towards you. As a child of the Father God, you are seen as pure, guiltless, holy, righteous, and faultless. Though your sins may have been many, He satisfied justice for each one on the cross. By receiving the gift of the Son of God, you have received eternal life! The life you now have is a righteous, pure, and holy life!

God wants us to express His holy life on the earth. **"Little children, let us not love in word or talk but in deed and in truth. 19 By this we shall know that we are of the truth and reassure our heart before him;"** (1 John 3:18-19) The Father helps us grow beyond just saying accurate things to actually doing the right things. He wants our hearts to confirm His liberating truth. **"for whenever our heart condemns us, God is greater than our heart, and he knows everything."** (1 John 3:20) It is good to recognize that our Heavenly Father knows better than us. If we find ourselves fluctuating in and out of faith, it helps to remind ourselves that He remains faithful. **"Beloved, if our heart does not condemn us, we have confidence before God;"** (1 John 3:21) God desires for us to engage with Him in confidence. He has opened the door wide for us to come to Him boldly. **"Let us then with confidence draw near to the throne of grace, that we may receive mercy and find grace to help in time of need."** (Hebrews 4:16) He wants us to have confidence so that we don't withdraw from Him and miss out on any good thing He has already made available to us through His Son. God has blessed us and wants us to experience all the good things that He has for us!

[7.3 That Whoever Believes In Him Should Not Perish]

Everyone of us deserves to perish in our sins, but God opened the way to escape through His Son Jesus. **"for all have sinned and fall short of the glory of God, 24 and are justified by his grace as a gift, through the redemption that is in Christ Jesus,"** (Romans 3:23-24) This is THE way to escape because it satisfies the legal demands of justice. Sin requires punishment. **"For the wages of sin is death, but the free gift of God is eternal life in Christ Jesus our Lord."** (Romans 6:23) Death is the punishment we have rightfully earned through our disobedience. Notice that eternal life is not something we can earn for ourselves. It is a gift, which by definition means, **"something given voluntarily without payment in return, as to show favor toward someone, honor an occasion, or make a gesture of assistance; present."** *Definition of gift | Dictionary.com. (2019). Www.dictionary.com.* https://www.dictionary.com/browse/gift In other words, we earned death through our disobedience, but Jesus earned life through His obedience. **"And being found in human form, he humbled himself by becoming obedient to the point of death, even death on a cross."** (Philippians 2:8) Because Jesus was the perfect sacrifice, Who died for us as one of us, God gained the full legal authority to forgive our sin when we receive the gift of eternal life in Christ Jesus. The required punishment for sin was fully paid by Jesus on the cross!

When we receive Jesus, we receive eternal life because the death we owe is completely satisfied by the death of Jesus. **"We know that our old self was crucified with him in order that the body of sin might be brought to nothing, so that we would no longer be enslaved to sin."** (Romans 6:6) Our receiving Jesus unifies us in His death, burial, and resurrection! **"I have been crucified with Christ. It is no longer I who live, but Christ who lives in me. And the life I now live in the flesh I live by faith in the Son of God,**

75

who loved me and gave himself for me."
(Galatians 2:20)

Now understand the contrast of the kingdom of darkness. Demons seduce people into doing bad things. They will incentivize people to make blood sacrifices in order to gain special knowledge and abilities which will give them an advantage over others in this life. People who crave occultic understanding will be drawn by demons to kill the most vulnerable. Babies have been sacrificed throughout history. They are most desired by evil spirits.

The spiritual side of darkness will become more detectable by those willing to commit the sacrifices they require. The physical person is tricked by the evil spiritual entity into shedding innocent blood which is something that the Lord hates. **"There are six things that the LORD hates, seven that are an abomination to him: 17 haughty eyes, a lying tongue, and hands that shed innocent blood, 18 a heart that devises wicked plans, feet that make haste to run to evil,"** (Proverbs 6:16-18) Shedding innocent blood becomes a pay-to-play scheme. Demons offer more mystical information to the individual in covenant with them who will purposefully do the things that God hates.

Many have made deals with darkness in darkness. In their prideful lust for power, they have turned themselves over to demons so that they can rise in influence. For special advantages so as to make inordinate amounts of ill-gotten wealth, they have networked with witches and warlocks. People wanting to acquire powers of darkness will be drawn to shed innocent blood either through abortions or some other ritualistic way. Through their multiplied blood sacrifices they attain mystical prowess in which they allow demons to express themselves through them as alter-egos. As unclean spirits cast spells through their willing hosts, they trigger effects in the blind masses mesmerizing them. This causes many of the world to listen to those who have done excessively evil things. Through the admiration of the world's populace, people become idolized and wealthy.

Justice is what the demons don't advertise much. They entice with money, power, and fame, while deemphasizing the everlasting punishment of sin. Some say that a loving God could not send people to hell. The truth is that people are already condemned and their liberation can only come through the Lord Jesus Christ. **"For God did not send his Son into the world to condemn the world, but in order that the world might be saved through him. 18 Whoever believes in him is not condemned, but whoever does not believe is condemned already, because he has not believed in the name of the only Son of God."** (John 3:17-18) People are condemned in their sins already! The love of God has been proven by the blood of Jesus! **"but God shows his love for us in that while we were still sinners, Christ died for us."** (Romans 5:8)

At most a person can only gain fame and fortune for the brief time they have on the earth. Even if that means living in luxury on the earth for 100 years, "...**what does it profit a man to gain the whole world and forfeit his soul?**" (Mark 8:36b) To lose your mind to depravity here and then be cast into the lake of fire forever is not worth anything offered by demons.

If you are reading this as one inspired to learn the way Christians fight spiritual warfare in order to counteract followers of Jesus, you need to repent. If you have sacrificed to demons you need to repent. There is good news for you. You can repent! The demonic realm may have convinced you that it is hopeless for you because you have done too many bad things, but God wants you to know that the blood of Jesus is stronger than any sin you committed! The blood of the Christ of God is stronger than all of your sins! This may be your last chance to turn from your wickedness. Don't forfeit your soul and live eternally separated from the love of God! Receive the blood of Jesus to wash over your sins! This is the gift of eternal life that God the Father offers you.

[7.4 But Have Everlasting Life]

The everlasting life of God is a gift that none of us deserve, but all of us can receive freely! God loves us so much that He paid the ultimate price so that we could be born again! Although we have all sinned, Jesus willingly paid for our sins by dying for them on the cross. This is good news!

If you have never received the gift of eternal life in Christ Jesus, now is the time. If you want to do that, pray this out loud, **"Father, I believe You love me and gave Your Son Jesus so that I could believe in Him and have eternal life. I believe in Jesus as my Lord and Savior. I believe Jesus died for my sins and was raised from the dead. I receive Jesus now! Amen."**

Soldiers of God, you carry the Father's heart. You have been given eternal life in Christ Jesus. You are empowered by the Holy Spirit. Now that you are in the Kingdom of light through receiving Jesus, you have a great commission. In Matthew 28:19-20, Jesus said, **"Go therefore and make disciples of all nations, baptizing them in the name of the Father and of the Son and of the Holy Spirit, 20 teaching them to observe all that I have commanded you. And behold, I am with you always, to the end of the age."**

Confessions for the Good Fight of Faith

The following confessions are for Kingdom Warriors. They are based on the instructions contained in this manual. Speak them out loud with the authority you have in Christ!

"I am not conformed to this world. I am transformed by the renewing of my mind!"

"I operate in the fruit of self-control through the power of the Holy Spirit!"

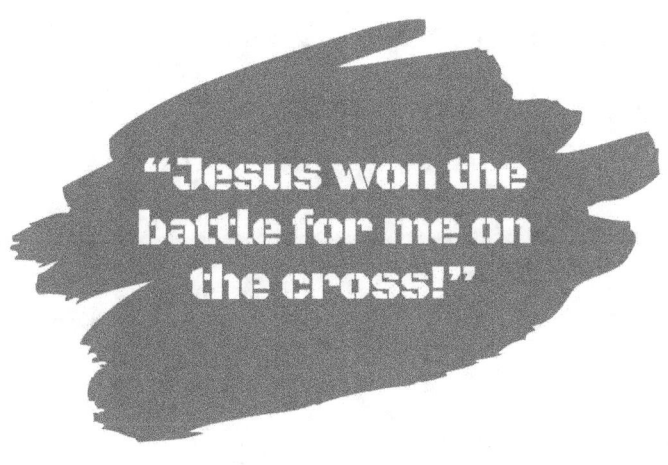

"Jesus won the battle for me on the cross!"

"God has given me a spirit of power, love, and a sound mind. I will not be intimidated by the enemy!"

"As a soldier of the Lord, I am on the side that has won, is winning, and will win!"

"For the Lord Most High is awesome. He is the great King of all the earth. He subdues the nations before us, putting our enemies beneath our feet."
[Psalm 47:2-3 NLT]

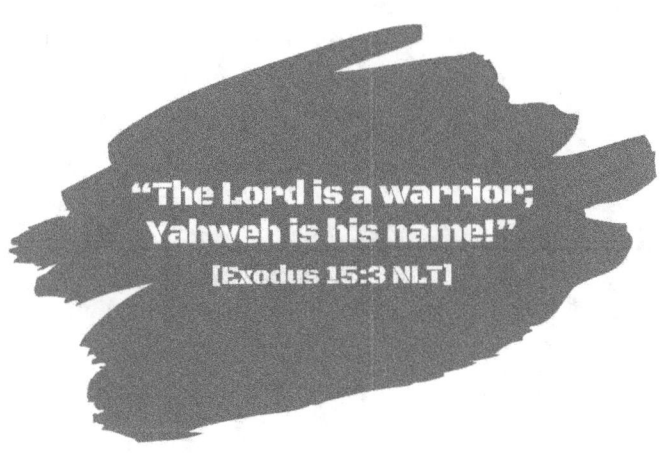

"The Lord is a warrior;
Yahweh is his name!"
[Exodus 15:3 NLT]

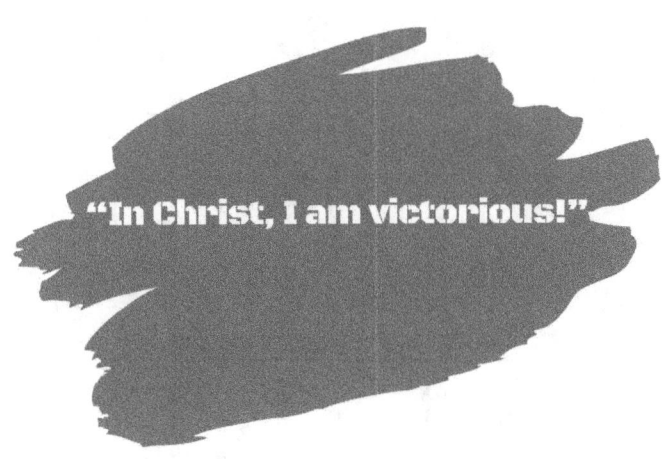

"In Christ, I am victorious!"

"I put on the full armor of God so that I can stand against the tactics of the Devil."

"I am more than a conqueror through the blood of Jesus Christ!"

"I cut through the lies of the enemy by wielding the sword of the Spirit!"

"For we do not wrestle against flesh and blood, but against the rulers, against the authorities, against the cosmic powers over this present darkness, against the spiritual forces of evil in the heavenly places."
[Ephesians 6:12]

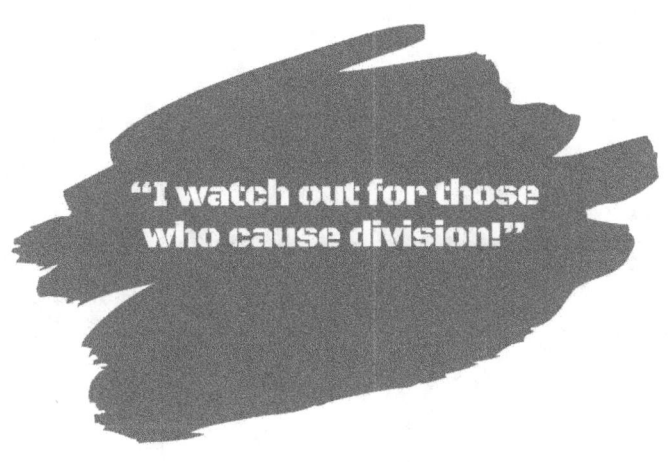

"I watch out for those who cause division!"

"True reality is revealed to me by the Holy Spirit."

"And be not drunk with wine, wherein is excess; but be filled with the Spirit;"
[Ephesians 5:18 KJV]

"He who dwells in the shelter of the Most High will abide in the shadow of the Almighty. I will say to the Lord, "My refuge and my fortress, my God, in whom I trust.""
[Psalm 91:1-2]

"The enemy cannot withstand the unified church that is flowing in the power of God!"

"For the Lord gives wisdom; from his mouth come knowledge and understanding;"
[Proverbs 2:6]

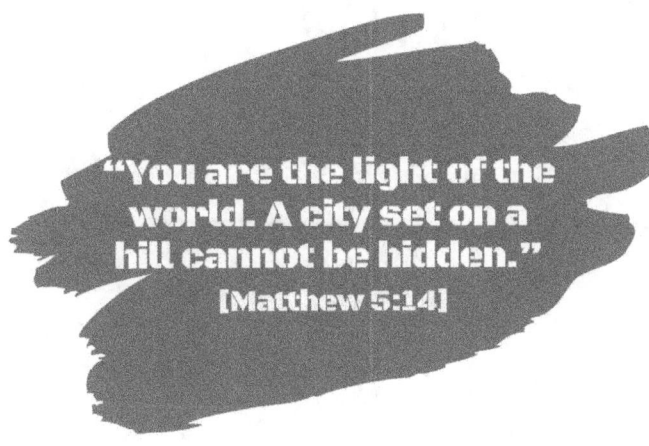

"You are the light of the world. A city set on a hill cannot be hidden."
[Matthew 5:14]

"The Holy Spirit gives me the divine strength to rise above sin!"

"But I say to you,
Love your enemies and
pray for those who
persecute you,"
[Matthew 5:44]

"I help liberate others
by sharing the good
news of Jesus Christ!"

"I am joined to the Lord and no devil destined for hell can disconnect my union with the Risen King!"

"The God of peace will soon crush Satan under your feet. The grace of our Lord Jesus Christ be with you."
[Romans 16:20]

"The Commander of Heaven's Army is also a great Father!"

"I choose to see myself the way my Father in Heaven sees me!"

"We know that our old self was crucified with him in order that the body of sin might be brought to nothing, so that we would no longer be enslaved to sin."
[Romans 6:6]

"I am a soldier of God who carries the Father's heart. I have been given eternal life in Christ Jesus and I am empowered by the Holy Spirit!"

Closing

The war has already been won. Jesus won the victory for us on the cross! As soldiers in the Kingdom of God we are victorious because of our Lord and Savior!

As we fight the good fight of faith through the power of God, it's important that we:

1. **Know God more.** (John 17)

2. **Believe who God says we are.** (2 Corinthians 5:17-21, Ephesians 1:3, 1 Peter 2:4-11)

3. **Gather with other soldiers of God.** (Hebrews 10:24-25, Ephesians 4:11-16)

God bless you warriors!

"And so, from the day we heard, we have not ceased to pray for you, asking that you may be filled with the knowledge of his will in all spiritual wisdom and understanding, so as to walk in a manner worthy of the Lord, fully pleasing to him: bearing fruit in every good work and increasing in the knowledge of God; being strengthened with all power, according to his glorious might, for all endurance and patience with joy; giving thanks to the Father, who has qualified you to share in the inheritance of the saints in light. He has delivered us from the domain of darkness and transferred us to the kingdom of his beloved Son," (Colossians 1:9-13)